WRITTEN IN THE STARS: A TEENAGE LOVE STORY

ROHAN SAHA

Made with ♥ on the Notion Press Platform
www.notionpress.com

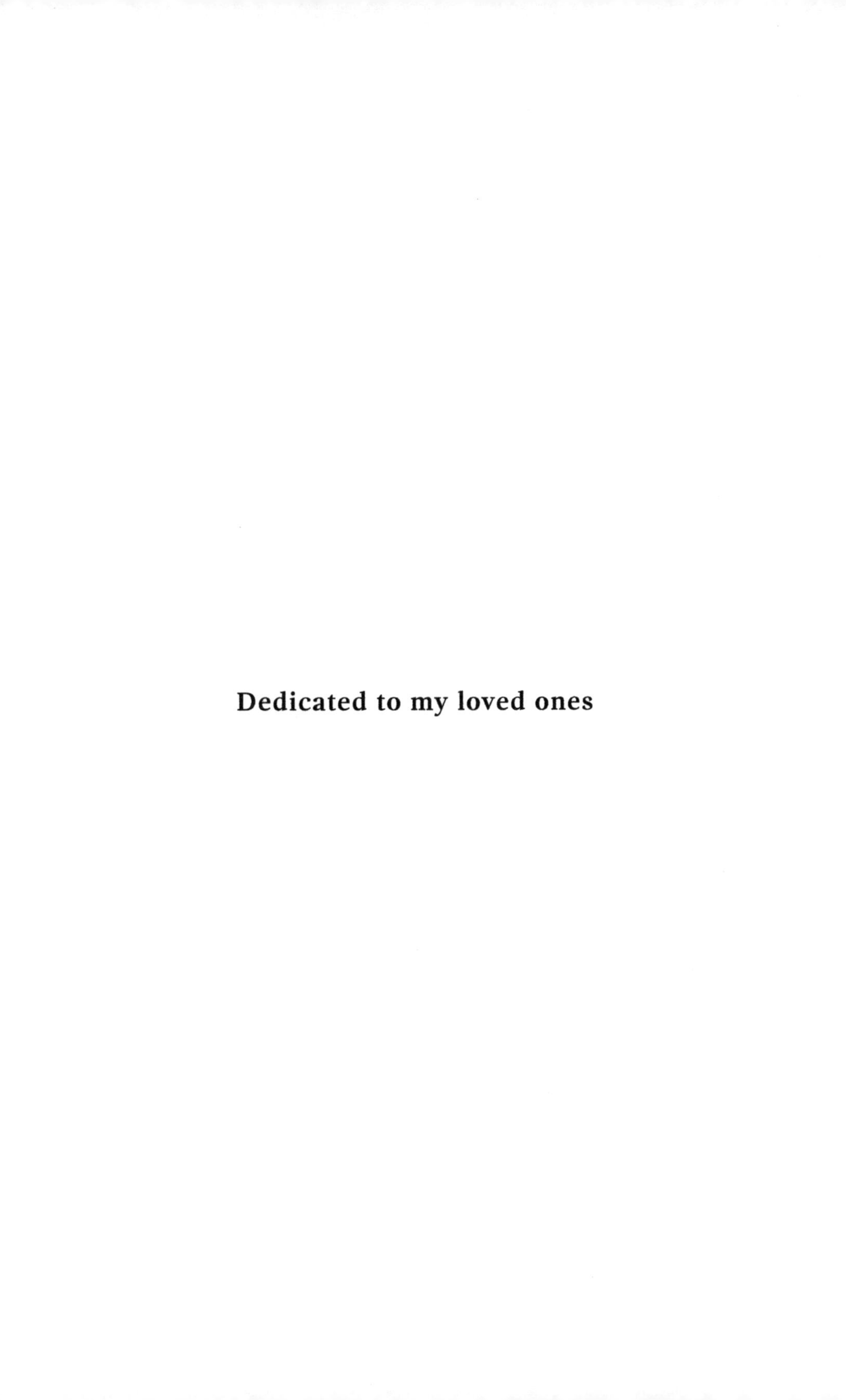

Dedicated to my loved ones

Contents

Contents

Written In The Stars: A Teenage Love Story

"Written in the Stars" follows the story of two teenagers, Lily and Alex, who meet by chance on a summer night and fall in love. As they navigate the ups and downs of a new relationship, they also explore their own identities and ambitions. With college looming in the near future, they must decide whether their love is worth pursuing or if it's better to part ways. Along the way, they learn valuable lessons about communication, trust, and self-discovery.

Title Significance:

The title "Written in the stars: A teenage love story" suggests that the love story of the teenagers in the book is destined to happen, as if it was written in the stars, and that their love is fated or predestined. It also implies a sense of romanticism and magic, as the idea of something being written in the stars is often associated with destiny and the universe. Overall, the title creates a sense of anticipation and wonder for the reader, implying that the love story will be an exciting and memorable journey for the characters involved.

CHAPTER ONE

Lily was feeling restless on that warm summer night. She had just finished her shift at the local ice cream parlor and was walking home, trying to shake off the exhaustion that had been building up in her body. As she walked down the quiet streets of her small town, she noticed a commotion up ahead. Curious, she walked closer to investigate.

It was a small crowd of teenagers gathered around a boy who was playing guitar on the sidewalk. Lily recognized him as Alex, a boy who was a few years older than her and went to a different school. She had seen him around town before, but had never actually spoken to him.

Alex was playing a song that Lily had never heard before, but she found herself entranced by the melody and the emotion in his voice. She walked closer and stood on the edge of the crowd, not wanting to draw attention to herself but unable to tear her eyes away from him.

When he finished the song, the crowd dispersed, leaving Lily standing alone. Alex looked up and caught her eye, and something in his expression made her heart skip a beat.

"Hey," he said, smiling at her.

"Hey," Lily replied, feeling suddenly shy.

They started talking, and soon they were deep in conversation, the kind that you can only have with someone you've just met. They talked about their dreams, their fears, and their favorite things. They laughed, and Lily felt a lightness in her chest that she hadn't felt in a long time.

As the night wore on, the conversation continued, and Lily and Alex found themselves drawn to each other in a way that neither of them could explain. They exchanged numbers and said goodnight, but Lily couldn't stop thinking about him as she walked the rest of the way home.

As she lay in bed that night, staring up at the ceiling, she realized that she had just had a chance encounter that might change the course of her life. She had met someone who had sparked something inside of her, and she couldn't wait to see what would happen next.

Lily woke up the next morning with a sense of excitement and anticipation. She wondered if Alex had thought about her as much as she had thought about him. She grabbed her phone and saw that he had sent her a text message.

"Good morning," it said. "Can't stop thinking about you."

Lily smiled to herself and started typing a response. She knew that this was just the beginning of something special, and she was ready to take the leap and see where it would lead.

CHAPTER TWO

Lily and Alex continued to talk and text after their chance encounter. They discovered they had a lot in common and enjoyed each other's company. Soon enough, they agreed to go on their first date.

For their date, Alex suggested they go for a hike in the nearby nature reserve. Lily had never been on a hike before, but she agreed, eager to try something new with him.

The hike was beautiful, with stunning views of the mountains and a cool breeze blowing through the trees. As they walked, they chatted easily, each one learning more about the other.

Lily felt comfortable with Alex, and he seemed to feel the same way. When they reached the summit, Alex pulled out a picnic blanket and some snacks he had packed in his backpack. They sat down and enjoyed the view while eating the food and talking some more.

As the sun began to set, they started packing up to head back down. Lily was feeling elated, and she realized that she really liked Alex.

On the way back down the trail, however, they hit a snag. Lily lost her footing and tumbled down a short embankment. Alex quickly ran to her side, and despite her protests, he insisted on carrying her down the rest of the trail.

Lily was embarrassed and a little scared, but Alex was kind and reassuring, telling her that it was no big deal and that he was glad to help. By the time they reached the bottom, Lily felt grateful for his chivalry and couldn't help but feel drawn to him even more.

As they said goodbye at the end of the date, Lily knew that she wanted to see him again. She felt a spark between them, and she couldn't wait to explore it further.

Over the next few weeks, they went on more dates, trying out different activities like visiting a local museum or going to a carnival. They had fun, but there were also some awkward moments, like when Lily accidentally spilled ice cream on herself or when Alex told a cheesy joke that fell flat.

Despite these minor hiccups, they continued to enjoy each other's company, growing closer with each passing day. Lily was impressed by Alex's kindness and sense of humor, and she found herself looking forward to his messages and calls.

As they got to know each other better, they started to let their guards down and reveal more of their true selves. They shared their hopes and dreams, their fears and insecurities. With each conversation, they felt more connected and more in tune with each other.

Lily couldn't help but feel like this was the start of something special, and she hoped that Alex felt the same way. She was excited to see where their relationship would go, and she was ready for whatever adventures and challenges lay ahead.

CHAPTER THREE

As Lily and Alex's relationship continued to blossom, they had to navigate the challenges of high school. They were both in different classes, had different friend groups, and had different extracurricular activities.

Despite these differences, they made an effort to spend time together, whether it was having lunch together, studying together, or attending each other's games and performances.

However, their relationship was not without its challenges. They faced gossip and rumors from their peers, who were jealous of their relationship or simply curious about their private lives. Lily and Alex tried to ignore the rumors and focus on their relationship, but it was difficult at times.

Moreover, Lily's parents were strict and protective, and they were not thrilled about their daughter dating someone they didn't know very well. They set rules and limitations on Lily's social life, which made it harder for her to spend time with Alex.

Alex, on the other hand, had a more laid-back family, who welcomed Lily into their home and treated her like a member of the family. This caused some tension between Lily and Alex, as she felt like he didn't understand the pressure and restrictions she was under.

Despite these obstacles, Lily and Alex remained committed to each other. They continued to support each other in their individual pursuits and looked for opportunities to spend time together outside of school.

One particularly challenging moment came when Alex's ex-girlfriend came back into the picture. Lily felt insecure and threatened by her, as she was older and more experienced than Lily. Alex reassured Lily that he was only interested in her, but the experience made Lily realize that she needed to work on her own self-confidence.

She started to focus on her own goals and interests, like joining a theater club and taking up photography. She also talked to Alex about her insecurities, which helped him understand her better and be more supportive of her.

As they navigated the ups and downs of high school, Lily and Alex's relationship grew stronger. They learned to communicate better, compromise, and trust each other. They also learned to value their own individuality and interests, while still making time for each other.

By the end of their high school years, Lily and Alex had become each other's best friend and confidante. They were ready to face the challenges of college and beyond, knowing that they had each other's backs.

CHAPTER FOUR

As Lily and Alex entered their college years, they started to explore their identities in new and exciting ways. They were both interested in social justice and activism, and they joined clubs and organizations that aligned with their values.

Lily started volunteering at a local homeless shelter, where she met people from all walks of life and gained a new perspective on poverty and inequality. She also started taking classes in gender and women's studies, which challenged her assumptions and broadened her understanding of gender and sexuality.

Alex, meanwhile, joined a political group on campus, where he advocated for environmental protection and social welfare. He also started taking classes in sociology and psychology, which helped him understand the complexities of human behavior and social structures.

As they pursued their interests and passions, Lily and Alex found themselves questioning their own identities and beliefs. Lily realized that she was attracted to people of different genders, which was a revelation for her. She struggled with coming out to Alex, but eventually, she mustered the courage to do so.

Alex was surprised at first, but he was also supportive and understanding. He loved Lily for who she was, regardless of her sexual orientation, and he wanted to learn more about the LGBTQ+ community.

This experience brought Lily and Alex even closer together, as they both opened up about their innermost thoughts and feelings. They continued to learn from each other and grow together, and they found new ways to express their love and affection.

One day, Alex surprised Lily with a homemade meal, complete with candles and flowers. He had also written her a poem, which he read to her as they sat together in his dorm room. Lily was moved to tears by the poem, which expressed his deep love and admiration for her.

In turn, Lily shared her own creative work with Alex, including a series of photographs she had taken that explored gender and sexuality. Alex was impressed by her talent and vision, and he encouraged her to pursue her art more seriously.

CHAPTER FIVE

Summer Love

As the school year ended and summer began, Lily and Alex found themselves facing a new challenge: a long-distance relationship. Lily was going to spend the summer with her family in another state, while Alex was staying in their college town to work and take classes.

At first, they were both apprehensive about being apart for so long. They had never been away from each other for more than a few days, and they didn't know how they would handle being in different states.

However, they were determined to make it work. They talked on the phone every day, sent each other messages and pictures, and made plans to visit each other during the summer.

Lily had a fun time with her family, but she missed Alex terribly. She found herself thinking about him all the time, and she couldn't wait to see him again.

One day, she received a surprise visit from Alex, who had driven all the way to see her. They hugged and kissed passionately, and it felt like no time had passed since they were last together.

They spent a week together, exploring the city, going on hikes, and spending lazy afternoons at the beach. They also had some intimate moments, which strengthened their bond and reignited their passion for each other.

However, they knew that their time together was limited, and that they would have to say goodbye soon. Lily felt sad and anxious about leaving Alex again, but he reassured her that they would be okay.

They continued to talk and stay in touch, and they planned more visits for the rest of the summer. They also made plans for the fall, when they would be reunited again at college.

As the summer drew to a close, Lily and Alex reflected on their relationship and their love for each other. They realized that distance had only made their love stronger, and that they were committed to each other no matter what.

On the last day of summer, Alex surprised Lily with a beautiful necklace, which he had designed himself. The necklace had a small pendant with their initials and a heart, symbolizing their love for each other.

Lily was moved by the gift, and she felt more in love with Alex than ever before. They hugged and kissed, knowing that they would soon be together again.

As Lily boarded the plane back to college, she felt grateful for the summer love that she and Alex had shared. She knew that they had something special and unique, and that their love was worth fighting for.

As they continued to explore their identities and interests, Lily and Alex also faced some challenges. They encountered people who were intolerant or judgmental of their beliefs and lifestyles, and they had to learn how to stand up for themselves and each other.

Despite these challenges, they remained committed to their relationship and to each other. They found strength in their shared values and beliefs, and they were excited to see where their exploration of identities would take them in the future.

CHAPTER SIX

The Future Looms

As Lily and Alex settled into their senior year of college, the future loomed large over them. They both had big decisions to make about their careers and their lives after graduation, and they weren't sure if they would be able to stay together.

Lily was applying to graduate programs in another state, and Alex had received a job offer in a different city. They had talked about their options and tried to come up with a plan, but they were both scared of what the future held.

They tried to focus on the present, enjoying their time together and making the most of their last year of college. They went on dates, spent time with friends, and took trips to nearby cities.

But the future still weighed heavily on their minds. They knew that they would have to make some tough decisions soon, and they didn't want to face the possibility of being apart.

One day, while taking a walk in the park, Lily and Alex talked about their fears and hopes for the future. They opened up to each other, sharing their deepest feelings and concerns.

Lily admitted that she was scared of leaving Alex behind, and that she wasn't sure if she could handle a long-distance relationship. Alex said that he felt the same way, and that he didn't want to lose Lily.

They both agreed that they wanted to try to stay together, but they didn't know how. They brainstormed different options, including moving together to a new city or finding a way to make a long-distance relationship work.

In the end, they decided to take a leap of faith and pursue their dreams together. Lily applied to a graduate program in the same city where Alex had received his job offer, and they started making plans to move in together.

It wasn't easy. They had to find a new apartment, adjust to a new city, and balance their new careers with their relationship. But they did it together, supporting each other through the tough times and celebrating the good times.

As they settled into their new life together, Lily and Alex knew that the future would still hold challenges. But they also knew that they had each other, and that their love would carry them through whatever came their way.

They continued to grow and evolve, both as individuals and as a couple. They faced new challenges, experienced new joys, and built a life together that was full of love and happiness.

Looking back on their journey, Lily and Alex knew that they had made the right decision. They had followed their hearts and taken a chance on love, and it had paid off in ways that they never could have imagined.

CHAPTER SEVEN

Making Tough Choices

As Lily and Alex continued to build their life together, they faced new challenges and tough choices. They had both been successful in their careers, but they were starting to realize that their paths were taking them in different directions.

Lily had always dreamed of being a professor and doing research, while Alex had discovered a passion for entrepreneurship and wanted to start his own business. They had talked about their goals and ambitions, but they weren't sure if they could make their dreams work together.

They knew that they would have to make some tough choices soon, and they didn't want to sacrifice their relationship for their individual goals.

One day, while sitting in their apartment, Lily and Alex talked about their future. They both agreed that they wanted to support each other's dreams, but they weren't sure if that was possible.

Lily was hesitant to give up her dream of becoming a professor, but she also didn't want to hold Alex back from pursuing his dreams. Alex felt the same way, and he didn't want to limit Lily's potential.

After much discussion, they came up with a plan. Lily would apply to a professorship program in a new city, and Alex would continue to work on his business. They would try a long-distance relationship for a year, and then reevaluate their situation.

It wasn't an easy decision, but they both knew that it was the right one. They supported each other from afar, sending texts, calls, and letters to stay connected.

As the year went on, Lily and Alex grew and evolved. They learned to communicate more effectively, and they started to understand each other's goals and passions on a deeper level.

At the end of the year, they came back together and reevaluated their situation. They both had made significant progress in their careers, and they knew that they still wanted to be together.

They came up with a new plan, one that would allow them to pursue their dreams together. Lily would continue her research and writing, while Alex would provide business guidance and support. They would work together to create a new kind of business, one that would combine their passions and talents.

It wasn't easy. They faced new challenges and obstacles, but they tackled them together, relying on their love and trust to guide them.

In the end, they succeeded. They created a thriving business that was both successful and fulfilling, and they did it together. They had made tough choices and sacrifices, but they knew that they had done it for each other, and for their shared future.

Looking back on their journey, Lily and Alex knew that their love had been the key to their success. They had learned to communicate, compromise, and support each other, and they had created a life that was full of happiness and purpose. They knew that they had made the right choices, and they were excited to see where their journey would take them next.

CHAPTER EIGHT

Epilogue

Lily and Alex's journey had been filled with ups and downs, but they had come out stronger and more in love than ever before. As they looked back on their life together, they knew that their love had been the key to their success.

They had built a successful business together, combining their passions and talents to create something unique and meaningful. They had faced challenges and obstacles, but they had tackled them together, relying on their love and trust to guide them.

Their love had also taken them on a journey of self-discovery and growth. They had learned to communicate more effectively, to compromise, and to support each other's dreams. They had navigated the complexities of their identities, and they had come out with a deeper understanding and appreciation of each other.

As they approached their anniversary, Lily and Alex decided to renew their vows. They invited their family and friends to a beautiful ceremony, where they declared their love for each other in front of everyone they cared about.

As they exchanged their vows, Lily and Alex knew that their love would continue to guide them. They were excited to see where their journey would take them next, and they were grateful for all the experiences that had led them to this moment.

In the years that followed, Lily and Alex continued to grow and evolve. They faced new challenges and obstacles, but they faced them together. They traveled the world, exploring new cultures and experiencing new adventures. They supported each other's dreams, and they built a life that was full of joy and purpose.

As they looked back on their life together, Lily and Alex knew that their love had been the foundation of their success. They had made tough choices, sacrifices, and compromises, but they had always done it for each other, and for their shared future.

They knew that their love would continue to grow and evolve, and they were excited to see what the future held. As they held each other close, surrounded by their loved ones, they knew that they were exactly where they were meant to be - together, forever.

Some Quotes That Touched My Heart And Will Touch Yours For Sure.....

1. "The best thing to hold onto in life is each other." - Audrey Hepburn

2. "Being deeply loved by someone gives you strength, while loving someone deeply gives you courage." - Lao Tzu

3. "I have waited for this opportunity for more than half a century, to repeat to you once again my vow of eternal fidelity and everlasting love." - Gabriel Garcia Marquez

4. "To be brave is to love someone unconditionally, without expecting anything in return." - Margaret Mitchell

5. "Love is not about how many days, months, or years you have been together. Love is about how much you love each other every single day." - Unknown

6. "The greatest happiness of life is the conviction that we are loved; loved for ourselves, or rather, loved in spite of ourselves." - Victor Hugo

7. "Love is not about possession. Love is about appreciation." - Osho

8. "Love is like the wind, you can't see it, but you can feel it." - Nicholas Sparks

9. "Love is not only something you feel, it is something you do." - David Wilkerson

10. "Love is not a matter of counting the years. But making the years count." - Michelle St. Amand

11. "The most important thing in life is to learn how to give out love, and to let it come in." - Morrie Schwartz

12. "Love is the voice under all silences, the hope which has no opposite in fear; the strength so strong mere force is feebleness: the truth more first than sun, more last than star." - E.E. Cummings

13. "The best love is the kind that awakens the soul and makes us reach for more, that plants a fire in our hearts and brings peace to our minds." - Nicholas Sparks

14. "I love you, not only for what you are, but for what I am when I am with you." - Elizabeth Barrett Browning

15. "When you love someone, you love the whole person, just as he or she is, and not as you would like them to be." - Leo Tolstoy

16. "Love is the flower you've got to let grow." - John Lennon

17. "I swear I couldn't love you more than I do right now, and yet I know I will tomorrow." - Leo Christopher

18. "I love you not because of who you are, but because of who I am when I am with you." - Roy Croft

19. "The best and most beautiful things in this world cannot be seen or even heard, but must be felt with the heart." - Helen Keller

20. "Love is not a feeling of happiness. Love is a willingness to sacrifice." - Michael Novak

9 798889 866756